For Zachariah, Eden, Lilly, Daphney, Hannah, and Gabriella
—A.J.L.

To each child who walks the path of creativity
and finds that it leads to the truth of who YOU are,
I say to you, right on! Be brave!
—R.G.

THIS IS A BORZOI BOOK PUBLISHED BY ALFRED A. KNOPF

Text copyright © 2019 by Andrea J. Loney
Jacket art and interior illustrations copyright © 2019 by Rudy Gutierrez

All rights reserved. Published in the United States by Alfred A. Knopf, an imprint of
Random House Children's Books, a division of Penguin Random House LLC, New York.

Knopf, Borzoi Books, and the colophon are registered trademarks of Penguin Random House LLC.

Visit us on the Web! rhcbooks.com

Educators and librarians, for a variety of teaching tools, visit us at RHTeachersLibrarians.com

Library of Congress Cataloging-in-Publication Data
Names: Loney, Andrea J., author. | Gutierrez, Rudy, illustrator.
Title: The double bass blues / by Andrea Loney ; illustrated by Rudy Gutierrez.
Description: First edition. | New York : Alfred A. Knopf, 2019. | Summary: After school orchestra
practice, young Nic carries his double bass through rough neighborhoods to his grandfather's home,
where he and Granddaddy Nic play jazz music with friends, delighting the neighbors.
Identifiers: LCCN 2017018472 (print) | LCCN 2017036505 (ebook) | ISBN 978-1-5247-1852-7 (trade) |
ISBN 978-1-5247-1853-4 (lib. bdg.) | ISBN 978-1-5247-1854-1 (ebook)
Subjects: | CYAC: Double bass—Fiction. | Musicians—Fiction. | Bands (Music)—Fiction. |
Grandfathers—Fiction. | Neighborhoods—Fiction. | African Americans—Fiction.
Classification: LCC PZ7.1.L6645 (ebook) | LCC PZ7.1.L6645 Dou 2019 (print) |
DDC [E]—dc23

The text of this book is set in Pluto Sans.
The artist used acrylic paint to create the illustrations for this book.
Designed by Martha Rago

MANUFACTURED IN THE U.S.A.

October 2019
10 9 8 7 6 5 4 3
First Edition

by **Andrea J. Loney**

DOUBLE
BASS
BLUES

illustrated by

Rudy Gutierrez

Alfred A. Knopf
New York

Hummmm . . .

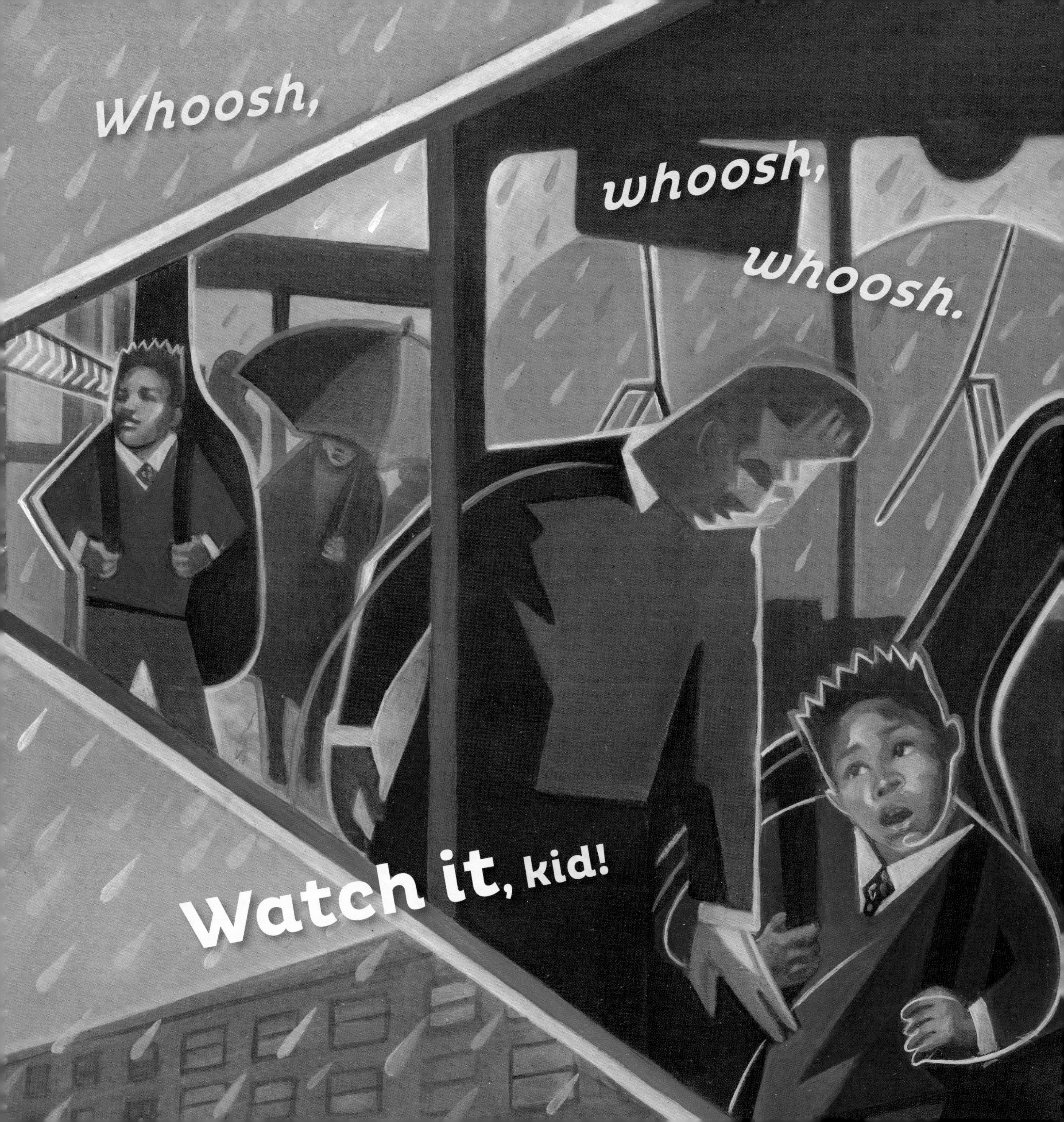
Whoosh,
whoosh,
whoosh.
Watch it, kid!

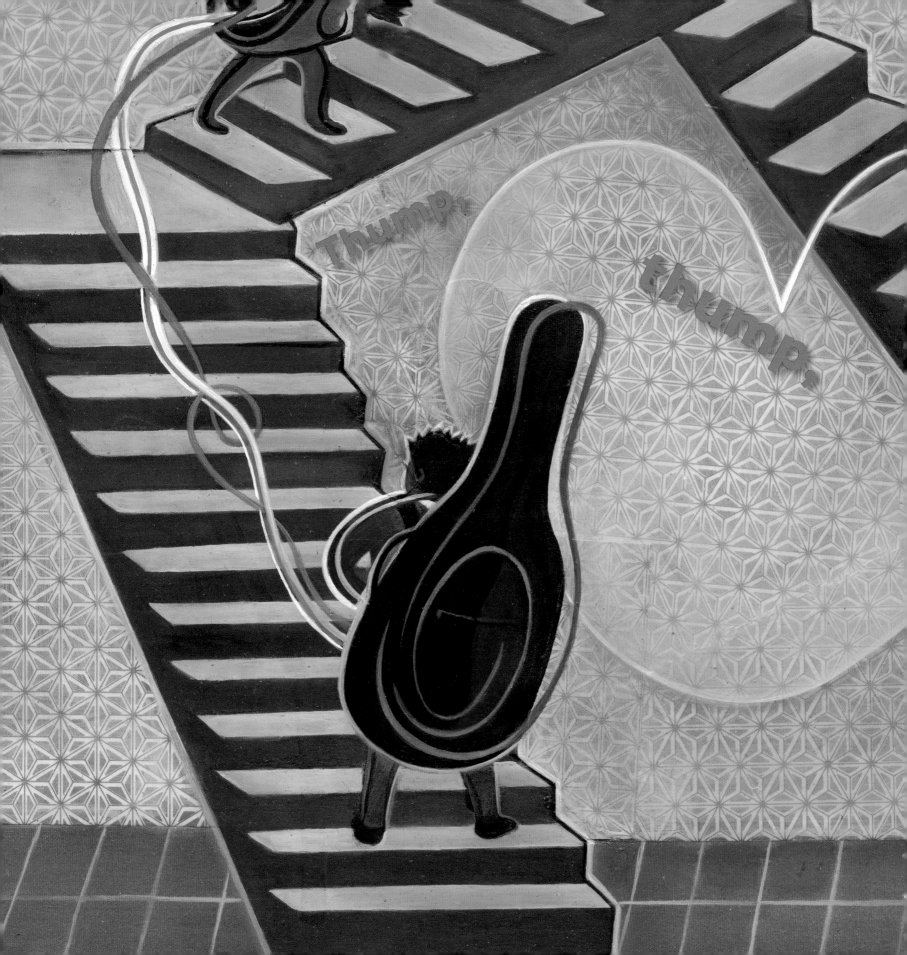

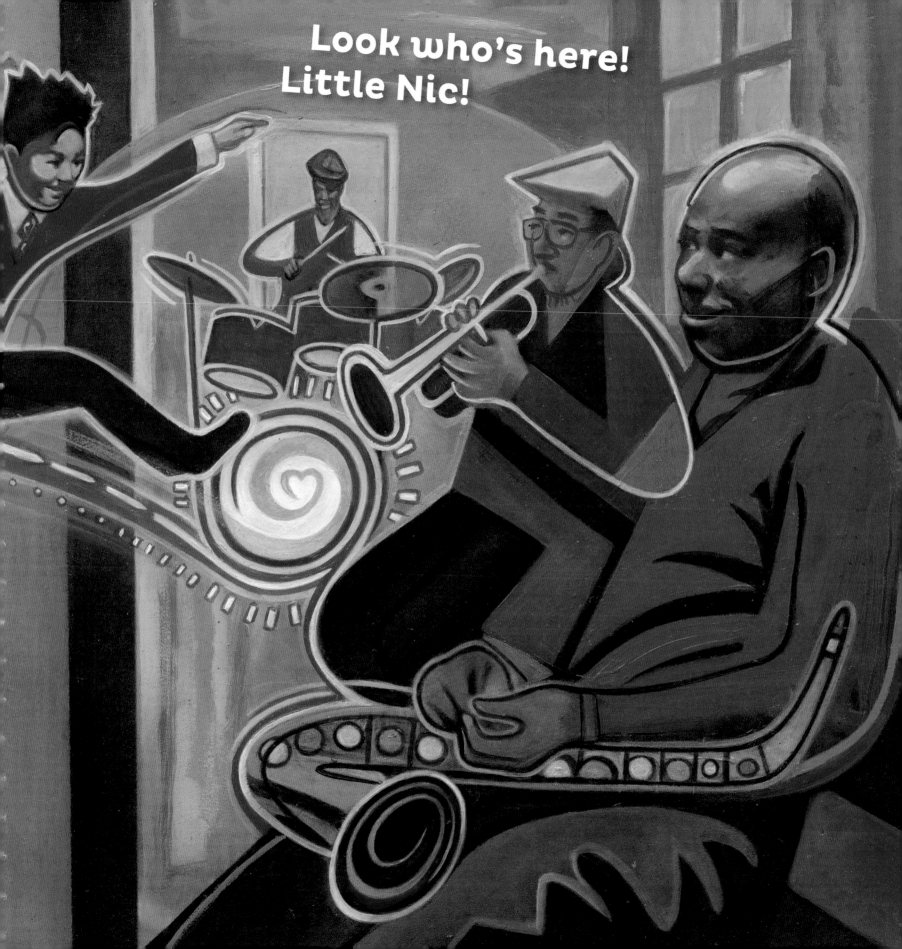

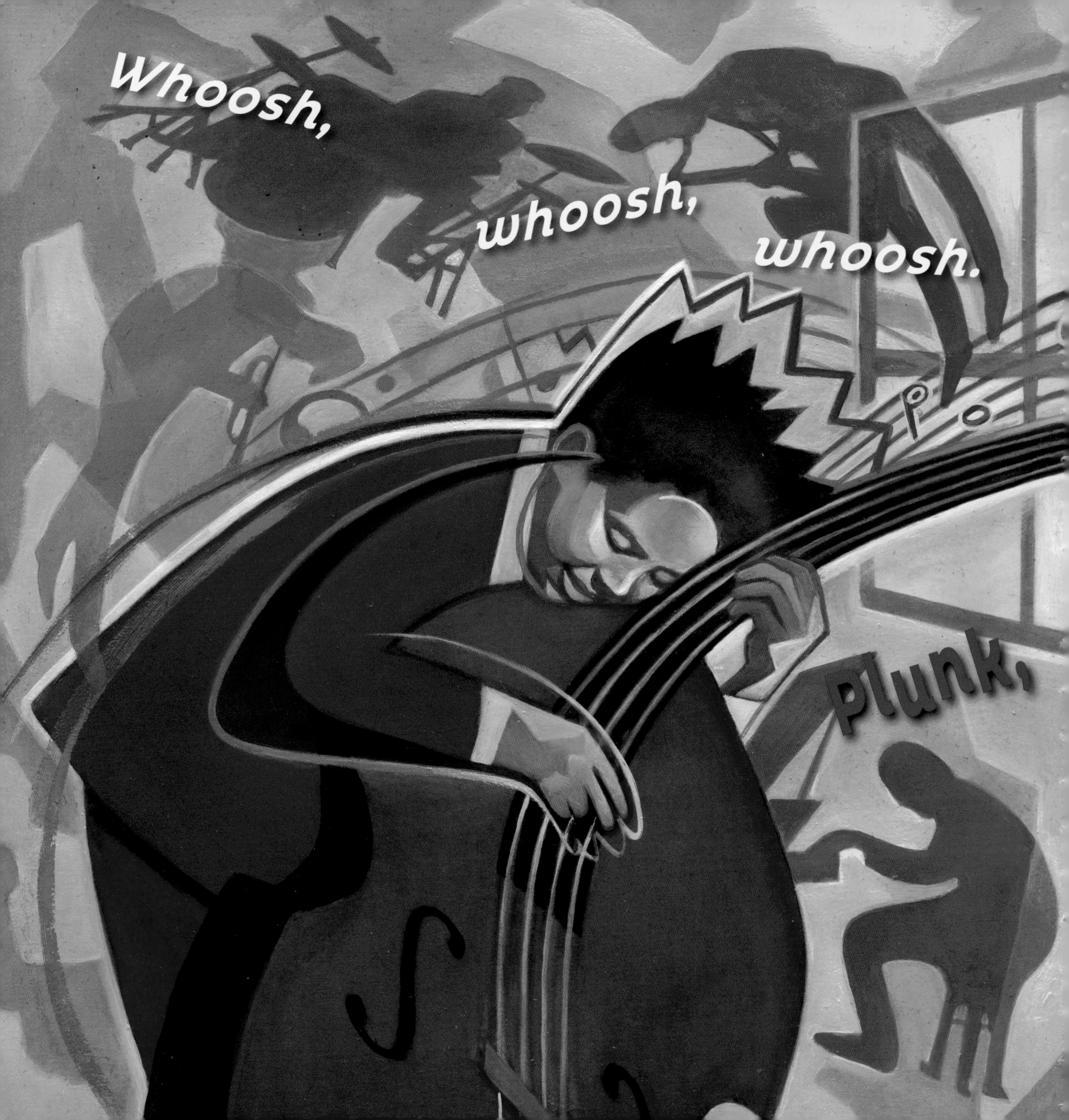
Whoosh,
whoosh,
whoosh.
Plunk,